I

ILL

For big bad Bryn
MD

BLOOMSBURY EDUCATION
Bloomsbury Publishing Plc
50 Bedford Square, London, WC1B 3DP, UK

BLOOMSBURY, BLOOMSBURY EDUCATION and the Diana logo are
trademarks of Bloomsbury Publishing Plc

First published in Great Britain 2019 by Bloomsbury Publishing Plc
Text copyright © Malachy Doyle, 2019
Illustrations copyright © David Creighton-Pester, 2019

Malachy Doyle and David Creighton-Pester have asserted their rights under the Copyright, Designs
and Patents Act, 1988, to be identified as Author and Illustrator of this work

A catalogue record for this book is available from the British Library

ISBN: PB: 978-1-4729-6250-8; ePDF: 978-1-4729-6251-5; ePub: 978-1-4729-6249-2
enhanced ePub: 978-1-4729-6955-2

2 4 6 8 10 9 7 5 3 1

Printed and bound in China by Leo Paper Products, Heshan, Guangdong

Chapter One

Big Bad Biteasaurus was the biggest baddest bully.
He frightened all the others with his big bad **BITE!**

He terrified the swimmers and the
hoppers and the crawlers.
Till Pete the tiny pterosaur squeaked,
"That's enough!"

Big Bad Biteasaurus looked up
and **ROARed!**

But Pete the tiny pterosaur dropped a
tree into his mouth.

Pete whistled up his friends.

Wheee!

And before Big Bad Biteasaurus could tear the tree from his own mighty jaws, everyone came and sat on him.

Chapter Two

The hoppers came, the crawlers came, even some of the swimmers came.

Until Big Bad Biteasaurus couldn't
move a big bad bit.

"Will you stop being such a big bad bully?" said Pete.

"GNUUH," said the massive dinosaur.

11

"I'll take that as a yes," said Pete.
"And will you stop all that roaring
and biting?"

Chapter Three

So the hoppers hopped, the crawlers crawled and the swimmers swam.

And what did Big Bad Biteasaurus do?

He chomped the mighty tree trunk.
And **PTHU!** He spat it on the ground!

Then he rose to all the bigness and the badness of his height.
He opened his enormo-saurus jaws and he **ROARed!**

"Can somebody just do something about these terrible teeth of mine? They're killing me!"

"You've got toothache?" said Pete. "You bet I have," moaned Big Bad Biteasaurus.

"Is that why you're
always so moody?"
said Pete.

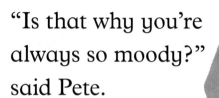

"You bet it is,"
groaned the
grumpy monster.

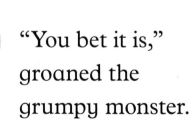

"If we can sort it out for you," said Pete,
"will you stop all that yelling?"

"You bet I will," said Big Bad
Biteasaurus.
"Do you promise?" said Pete.
"Cross my big bad dinosaur
heart," said Big Bad Biteasaurus.

"Well first we'd better clean up those terrible teeth of yours," said Pete. "They're disgusting!"

So he whistled up his friends again.
"Wheee!"
And back they hopped, crawled
and swam.

Chapter Four

They were still a bit scared, especially the tiniest ones, but they started picking out the mucky stuff from the monster's yucky teeth.

Pickety-pluck, scrapity-scrape, polishy-polish. Till Big Bad Biteasaurus positively beamed!

Then Dot, the dinosaur dentist,
took a look.
"I can see the rooting-tooting problem,"
she said. "Rotten teeth! Hold steady,
big fellow!"

So everybody held on tight, to stop
Big Bad Biteasaurus from wriggling
and jiggling, while Dot the dinosaur
dentist got to work.

"Clean them every day!" she told him,
when she was done. "And stop eating
rubbish!"

Now Big Bad Biteasaurus isn't a
great scary bully any more...

Though sometimes he does like to show off his clean and shiny teeth (the ones he's got left).